Hairy Fairy

G. H.

Scholastic Children's Books,
Commonwealth House, 1-19 New Oxford Street,
London WC1A 1NU, UK
a division of Scholastic Ltd

London ~ New York ~ Toronto ~ Sydney ~ Auckland
Mexico City ~ New Delhi ~ Hong Kong

First published by David Fickling Books, an imprint of Scholastic, 2001
This edition published by Scholastic Ltd, 2001

Text and illustrations copyright © Sue Heap 2001

ISBN 0 439 99861 1 (Hardback) 0 439 99388 1 (Paperback)

Printed and bound in China

Hairy Fairy

Sue Heap

Once upon a time
there was a little fairy.
Her hair was short
and sharp and spikey!

Little Fairy went to see
her friend, Big Fairy.

"I'll make your wish come true!"
said her friend, Big Fairy.

Big Fairy danced up.

Big Fairy danced down.

. . . with her feet in the air
and her head on the ground as
the magic went round and
round and faster and
faster and faster
until she just couldn't stop
and then with a bang,

the magic went

POP!

Oh no!

Little Fairy's hair has turned
big, bushy, thick and green!

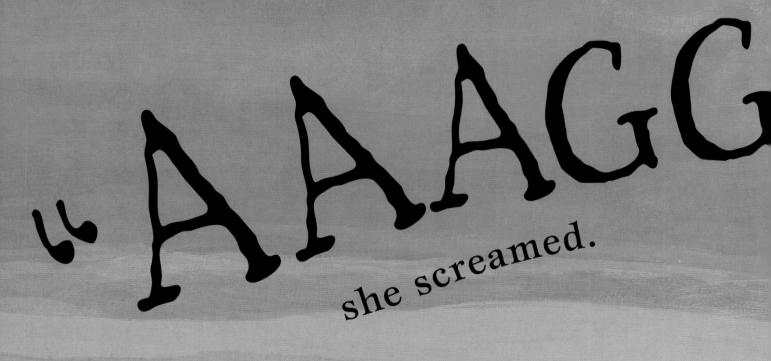

"AAAGG

she screamed.

HHH!"

"Look what you've done!"
she said.

"It's not that bad,"
said Big Fairy, "mmm,
I think it looks lovely!"

"OK, then!" said Little Fairy.
"I'll do your hair!"

Little Fairy buzzed up.

Little Fairy buzzed down.

and the magic went round and round

and faster
and faster

until she just couldn't
stop and then with a bang,

the magic went
POP!

Oh no!

Big Fairy's hair has turned pointy, sharp and green! "OOOOHHHH!!" she screamed. "Look what you've done!" cried Big Fairy.

"It's not that bad," giggled Little Fairy. "Mmm, in fact I like it!" she said.

"Thanks a lot!" said Big Fairy, and she started to cry.

"Well. I don't like my hair either!" said Little Fairy.

'It's not what I wished for at all!"

"I want my hair like it was before," said Big Fairy.

"I know, let's do a dance and make it better," she said.

So the fairies danced up and
the fairies danced down!

And the magic went round
and round and faster
and faster until they
just couldn't stop and

then with a bang,
the magic went
POP!

Ahhhhhhhhhhh!!! Big Fairy's hair is just as it was before, long and wavy and black!

Ooooohhhhhhh!!! Little Fairy's wish has come true! Her hair is long and curly and twirly!

Little Fairy and Big Fairy went
up and down the hill, dancing
and laughing all the way home.

"What if I made your nose a little bit longer," said Little Fairy . . .

"Well then, I could make your bottom bigger and better," said Big Fairy . . .

And that is the
end of this happy,
hairy, fairy tale.